All About My Selfie

Shannon Freeman

SADDLEBACK
EDUCATIONAL PUBLISHING

The Most Beautiful Bully

Silentious

The Alternative

All About My Selfie

www.sdlback.com

ISBN-13: 978-1-68021-009-5
ISBN-10: 1-68021-009-2
eBook: 978-1-63078-291-7

Printed in Guangzhou, China
NOR/0515/CA21500758

19 18 17 16 15   1 2 3 4 5

Acknowledgements

I have been so inspired by all the wonderful posts that fill my newsfeed daily. Just know that those who inspired this story also bring joy to so many who read your posts. You are content generators. Where would social media be without you?

I have to acknowledge my dear sister-in-law Marcie Freeman, who has inspired my characters in former books and this one. You have an eye for content! Keep the posts coming, and I will continue to read.

Shannon Galvan, I would expect nothing less. You've had us doubled over since high school. Good reads! Good reads!

I would like to thank Misty Williams. My classmate, you are hilarious and missed your comedic calling. You keep us all laughing.

As for Darrell Smothers, one word: lol. You keep social media entertaining!

Thank you, Carol Pizer! You know and I know what that means. You are truly a great editor. You will forever be a part of my story.

Thank you to Tim and Arianne McHugh. You are truly trailblazers in this industry. I can't say enough how blessed I am to be a part of your vision. This is a dream come true.

I love my family! You are supportive beyond measure. Derrick Freeman, Carolyn Warrick, Rochelle Jenkins, Deborah Freeman, Felisha Collins, and Shannon Richard. My life works because you are a part of it. I love you all!

Dedication

To the educators who put your students' needs before your own on a daily basis. Sometimes it can be a thankless job. So, thank you for all you do for the next generation.

Chapter 1

The Swansons

*E*mma Swanson was always trying to find her place in Texsun City. It wasn't her fault that she'd been shunned by her peers. She wasn't sure who to blame. She just knew she didn't measure up somehow.

Her family had money and beachfront property. Emma had every luxury a girl could want. But it wasn't enough. She'd tried out for cheerleading twice. She didn't make the cut either time. Then she gave up trying to be popular. She was over trying to fit in.

Instead, she tried to find things that interested her. Like art or horseback riding. She wasn't seeking anyone's approval. It didn't matter.

She heard the rumors about her grandfather's fortune. How other families had not been as successful. It was easy to blame him. Nobody complained when the rice industry was booming. Money grew on trees. Then taxes took their toll. Some found it hard to stay afloat. But not Emma's grandfather.

Thomas Swanson had been a smart man. He was able to spread his money around. In other words, he hid it. Then he bought out his partners. He passed his fortune down to his children.

Many resented his quick thinking. Some moved on to different businesses. Others just went under. Emma didn't know how much of the story was true. She believed some of it had to be. She loved her grandfather. He was shrewd. He knew how to handle money. One thing was for sure, he loved his family. That was what mattered to Emma.

Unfortunately, his dealings with his former rivals made Texsun City a difficult place to live for Emma. And made Summit Middle School especially tough. Emma could ask him to donate money to build a better library. Or ask him to make some grand gesture that would create goodwill. Grease the path for her. But she didn't want to. She wanted to be accepted for who she was. If the other girls wanted to hate her because of family rivalry, then so be it. She knew one day she would figure it out on her own.

When Carson Roberts showed up at Summit Middle School, Emma found "her tribe." The girls instantly hit it off. Who knew opening Summit to so many new faces would be Emma's salvation? It was just what she needed. And at the perfect time.

Carson was a breath of fresh air. They had a common enemy. And they found a kindred spirit in Mai Pham. Emma had known Mai for many years. But they had never really opened up to each other. Each was dealing with her own walls, built to protect them from the SMS mean-girl cliques.

"Emma! Come downstairs, darling," Miss Arina called.

Miss Arina was Emma's rock. She had been her nanny since infancy. She was the constant in her world. Her nanny got Emma through the hard times. Her parents had a lot on their plate. Her father ran Swanson Rice. Her mother worked tirelessly with Texsun City nonprofits.

Emma ran down the staircase to her

nanny. Miss Arina's solid frame was waiting in the foyer, wearing a starched white apron over her clothes.

"Your father just arrived in town," she said in her heavy Russian accent. "Your parents are taking you out for dinner tonight. You need to get ready."

"Mommy and Daddy?"

"Yes, dear. Now go get pretty, please. Put on something that makes those green eyes pop."

Miss Arina hugged Emma tightly. Then she retreated into the kitchen.

Emma returned to her room. She looked through her closet, debating what to wear. She already knew where they were going to eat. Whenever her parents called for dinner out, they sat down at Sartain's.

Where else did people from Texsun City go when they all got together? Sartain's wasn't fancy, but it was good. They had the best barbequed crabs in the area. You could eat as much as your stomach could handle. Plus, Sartain's was mellow. They would be able to talk. Catch up on their lives.

Emma decided to go casual. She slipped on her green cashmere sweater, skinny jeans, and brown Uggs. She was ready for some barbequed crabs.

When the limousine arrived in the circular driveway, Miss Arina called for her. Emma ran to meet her parents, who were waiting patiently for their only child. Her father hugged her tightly. Her mother watched her with loving eyes.

"How's my girl?" she asked when Emma was allowed to come up for air.

"I'm fine, Mom. Are you here for a while this time?"

"I am, darling. Thank God."

They talked until they pulled up at

Sartain's. They were seated immediately. Then they ordered. The family continued catching up while they ate. Their fingers tingled from all of the wonderful, finger-licking spices.

"It's good to be back in Texas," her father announced.

"Yes it is," Mrs. Swanson agreed. "So how is Mai doing with her singing?" she asked Emma.

"She's fine. We have a few shows coming up soon. And I wanted to ask a favor of you both."

"Anything, dear," her father replied.

"Well, I wanted to see if it would be okay for Mai to perform at the Rice Festival this year."

"That's an excellent idea," her mother said approvingly.

"We have some big names coming into town for that," her father said. "But I'm sure we can add her to the roster. We'll find a place."

"Oh, thanks, Dad. She is going to be thrilled. I can't wait to tell her."

They continued eating until they couldn't possibly eat another crab. They sat stuffed in their chairs, vowing that they needed a month to recover before they could return to their favorite family restaurant.

Chapter 2

My, My Mai

During their next meeting, Elise Mitchell laid out plans for Mai's singing career. Elise was Summit's supreme It girl. The most popular and smartest girl in school. She was going places. And she was taking Mai with her.

Mai's spring semester was booked, thanks to Elise's management. Elise planned a few summer shows too. Carson, Emma, and Mai knew this was going to be a hectic time for them. But the focus and pressure was on

Mai. Elise wanted her performing as much as possible. The more shows she did, the more videos they could cut and splice. This gave them a product to sell. Elise's intent was on getting Internet time.

"Look, we can't go on tour like most people. We have to work with what we have. Right now, we work Texsun City and the surrounding areas. We use the Internet to our advantage. Then the audience will come to us," Elise said.

Carson and Emma were working hard on Mai's behalf. Elise called a meeting every day. Or it seemed like she did. Sometimes the three girls thought Elise just liked to hear herself talk. But they had to admit, she was definitely helping Mai.

Elise was the student body president. She took her job seriously. When she approached Mai to handle her singing career, Mai didn't hesitate to accept. Any job she took, Elise was all in. She expected the people around her to be the same way.

Elise wanted them to think about Mai's career 24/7. And Mai was their friend, so they gave it their all. But Elise always wanted more. It was frustrating at times. Mai was happy, though. The last thing Emma and Carson wanted to do was to complain about Elise.

"My parents agreed to find a place for Mai to perform at the Rice Festival," Emma announced.

The Rice Festival was one of the largest fairs in the area. It attracted some of the hottest performers to Texsun City.

"That's awesome, Emma!" Mai said excitedly, looking at her with big round eyes. "Wow! Thank your parents for me, please."

Emma smiled, happy she could contribute. "You can do it yourself. I'll definitely give them the message, though.

"Okay, we have a lot of work to do to prepare for the Rice Festival. That's no small thing," Elise warned them.

"I know that, Elise," Emma snapped. Elise had said it as if Emma was clueless. As if she'd never attended the Rice Festival. It was her family's baby. She knew more than anyone about how much work would be required to pull off a performance at the event. She had lived it.

"I know you know, Emma. You don't have to be ugly. I was just trying—"

"I don't think Emma meant it like that," Carson said, trying to stop a verbal sparring match. "I think what she was trying to say is that she's been a part of the Rice Festival for a long time, and—"

"Don't speak for me, Carson," Emma told her. "Elise, you come across as a know-it-all. We all have something to give."

Mai had to step in. "Emma, I appreciate

what everybody's bringing to the table. Nobody's being paid to be here. I just appreciate what y'all are doing. I don't know if I've said it lately, but thank you. All of you. Seriously, I couldn't do this without you. Now let's get through these next shows. Are we good?" she asked her team.

Emma had to admit, Mai knew exactly what to say. It was that leadership quality that made Mai a star. Emma wished she could be so tactful, so calming. Instead, she seemed to be the one always putting her foot in her mouth.

Elise spoke up. "Hey, I just want what's best for Mai. That's all."

"Me too," Emma said defensively. She could feel the room tighten again. *What is wrong with me? Calm, Emma, calm.* She took a deep breath, trying to let out the bad air she'd gulped down.

"We all want what's best for Mai,"

Carson said, grabbing her friends and bringing them in for a hug.

Carson was the glue. Mai was the star. And Emma? She was still unsure what her role was. She went in for the hug. But her heart wasn't at peace. She had to figure this out. She had to find out who she was. She knew if she didn't, she would come apart at the seams. She could feel Elise looking at her, as if she could read her mind.

They went back to planning mode after everything had been ironed out. The district-wide talent show was the first event. It was being held at Summit. Mai simply had to win. She couldn't come in second to anyone. It would ruin her image. The team had to be on point. Carson was handling lighting and cues. Elise would be in charge of set design. Emma had to get the costume ready.

The day of the show, they were all on

edge. They went to their classes. But they could barely focus. There were so many details. So many things needed to be handled just right. Math class didn't seem as important.

They rushed through their assignments and met up in the auditorium.

"Hey, I can't get in touch with the guy who's supposed to bring the dry ice," Elise told them. It was one hour before showtime. "She can't be a genie without smoke. There's just no way." Elise tried her cell phone.

Emma picked up the phone and made a call. She walked across the stage as she spoke. When she returned, she said, "Dry ice is on the way."

"Well, I guess being a Swanson does have its perks," Elise said sarcastically.

"What is that supposed to mean?" Emma asked with frustration.

Elise rolled her eyes and turned away. It was a constant battle between Elise and

Emma. Mai was always the girl stuck in the middle.

Mai grabbed Emma's arm as she turned to go after Elise. "Don't, please." She looked deep into Emma's eyes. "Just let it go, for me." Emma nodded. She would finish with Elise later. "Thanks for getting the dry ice," Mai told her.

"Don't tell Elise. I just called Miss Arina. She said she'd do anything for her favorite performer."

Mai laughed. And Elise thought she had some big connections! Emma had called her nanny. Miss Arina loved Emma. And anyone who loved Emma. That meant both of Emma's besties: Mai and Carson.

Mai's talents were uncovered at a sleepover at Emma's house. From that day on, Miss Arina declared herself Mai's number one fan. Now she was coming through in a tense situation.

The performance was much better than the preparation leading up to it. Mai turned on her talent as soon as the microphone was in her hand. She was the last act. She brought down the house. The audience was on its feet, applauding wildly. Her friends beamed with pride backstage. One thing could not be denied: Mai Pham was a star.

"Mai, Mai, Mai!" the audience chanted as she held the first place trophy high over her head.

"Thank you!" she yelled into the mic. It was her moment.

Chapter 3

The Rice Festival

*E*mma's house was packed with supplies for the Rice Festival. Miss Arina wore many hats in the Swanson family household. And this week she was the main organizer.

"I cannot wait until this week is over," she told Emma. The two were working on ribbons for the Swanson Rice float.

"Really? But it's so fun. The Rice Festival is part of who I am. I've been on these floats since I was two years old."

"I know. I was the one holding you. Don't you remember?"

"Of course I do," Emma said, nestling close to Miss Arina.

"Emma!" her mother called. "We have to go. Dad is going on stage in the next hour to announce the bands. He wants us to be with him."

"I'm sorry I can't stay to help," she told Miss Arina.

"This is almost done. You go have fun. Is everything ready for Mai's performance today?"

"Yes, ma'am. I'm bringing the costumes now." She hugged Miss Arina and ran downstairs to help her mother.

"I'm ready," Emma said to her mom. She was dressed warmly. And she wore only black to blend in with the rest of Mai's team.

Her mother was wearing her cream wool coat with fur trim and matching hat and gloves. She looked every bit like the woman of the hour.

"Darling, you can't wear that on the stage. You look adorable. This is your father's event, though. Go upstairs and change."

"Mom, I have to work today. Mai is performing."

"Today is for our family. We *let* Mai perform. That shouldn't take you away from your family duties. You'll be on the head float when she's singing. Now get Miss Arina to give you the outfit I bought for you."

Emma felt torn as she ran upstairs. She had warned Mai that she would have a lot on her plate on the festival's opening day. But Mai had begged Emma to be by her side. She was nervous. She had never performed in front of such a large crowd. Emma had promised she would be there for her.

But she couldn't disappoint her parents. They counted on her too.

"Miss Arina!" she called out. "Mom wants me to change my clothes. She thinks I'm much too *plain* to represent the family."

"No problem. I know exactly what she wants you to wear." Miss Arina unzipped the black bag that hung in her large walk-in closet. Inside was the most beautiful wool coat Emma had ever seen. It was emerald green and fitted at the top. It was nipped at the waist. The bottom of the coat fell in a soft A-line, giving Emma the illusion of having curves.

Her mother knew Emma's style. She had also selected a pair of khaki pants with a hint of shine, an ivory cashmere sweater, and new brown riding boots. Dangling from the hanger were new pearl earrings and a pearl necklace. Emma ran her fingers across the pearls.

"Do you like it?" her mother's voice said from behind her.

"I love it," Emma whispered.

"I knew you would. Hurry and change

your clothes. Daddy already called to see if we were en route."

Emma dashed inside her closet for a quick change. When she was done, she looked every inch her mother's daughter. The green and ivory complimented her mother's coat perfectly. Her mom had an undeniable eye for fashion. She was savvy and it showed. She was Texas-born. But that didn't hold her back from visiting New York and Paris.

Emma's mother's style changed depending on her mood. One day she looked sophisticated and elegant. The next day she looked breezy and relaxed. Today, her look could give the First Lady a run for her money. She wore her red hair straight. She looked polished and calm.

Emma quickly gathered her hair into a sleek bun to give herself the same polish.

"You look absolutely amazing," her

mother said. "The bun was a great touch. It will last through the parade. That wind can be brutal."

"Thanks, Mom."

Emma was still torn between her family's float and Mai. She snapped a selfie before leaving her room. Then she posted it to Friender with the caption "Rice Festival, here I come."

"Mom, take an 'usie' with me," she pleaded.

"Oh, you're into taking pictures now? Please! You always hated pictures. Almost as much as I hate social media. Just promise not to post it."

"Okay, okay." They captured the moment and headed to the door.

She could hear the festival before she could see it. Carnival rides. Crowds of people. Food trucks. Arcade games. Their car turned the corner. Emma looked out the window.

Instantly, butterflies swirled in her stomach. She gulped.

"I'm so nervous," she said as she saw the crowds. The stage was swarming with people.

"You don't even have to speak. We are just there to support your father."

Their driver, Mr. Victor, pulled the car up to VIP parking. Emma and her mother got out. Mrs. Swanson asked the driver to bring Mai's costumes to the dressing area.

A VIP tent was stocked with swag. There was something for everyone.

The festival hosted a variety of performers. There was so much talent in Texsun City. All had agreed to come and perform. On opening day, there was a mix of music groups: country, rap, pop, and gospel. They were all waiting for their turn on stage.

Mr. Swanson greeted Emma and her

mother at the entrance of the tent. Then he led them to their section. "My beautiful girls are here," he said, hugging each of them.

"Daddy, have you seen Mai?"

"Of course. Her dressing area is right next to us. I knew you'd want her close."

Emma couldn't help it. She had to go find her friends. She couldn't wait to show them the clothes and jewelry her mom had bought for her. This was the first year she was truly excited about the Rice Festival.

"Mai?" she asked timidly, peeking into her friend's dressing area.

Mai sat in a large chair. Someone was doing her makeup. Carson was standing next to her. Elise was pacing off to the side.

"Emma, where are the costumes?" Elise asked as soon as she saw her.

"Our driver should be here in a minute. He's bringing them over."

"Um, great! You show up late and with no costumes."

Emma pictured this moment going much differently. There was no way she was about to be sucked into another argument with Elise. She just had to ignore her.

"Hey, Elise, back off," Mai said. "The costumes are here. They're just not in *here*. It's fine, they—"

Before she could complete her sentence, one of the stagehands entered with a black garment bag. Mai's costumes had arrived.

Emma didn't speak. She gave Elise a sideways glance and moved to Mai's side. "So how are you doing? Nervous at all?"

"That's not even the word. I think my bones are shaking," she said anxiously.

"Oh, you'll be fine. You always are."

"That's what I've been trying to tell her," Carson said, agreeing with Emma.

Mrs. Swanson appeared in the doorway. She beckoned her daughter to join her. Then she left.

"Hey, I have to go. My father's making the opening statements."

Carson stopped her. "Em, you look beautiful," she said, winking at her best friend.

"Thanks, Carson."

Emma could feel her knees wobbling as she walked up the five steps that led to the stage. She had a clear view of her parents. They were both so regal and comfortable in front of an audience. Her father's voice was clear and commanding. She was always so proud of him. Her mother was standing by his side. She looked loving and supportive.

Emma went to her. She grasped her hand. Her mom gave her a reassuring squeeze during her father's speech.

"Now let's hear some music!" her father

yelled in his best Texas drawl. The crowd erupted, whooping and clapping.

Just like that, it was over. Emma had lived through it. She took a deep breath. She felt like she didn't breathe during her father's speech. It was as if she was oxygen-deprived for the last five minutes.

She walked into the VIP tent. She got a drink and a sandwich from a beautifully decorated buffet table. As soon as she got her nerves under control, she went to check on Mai.

Mai's makeup was finished. She was ready to put on her outfit. Emma had chosen it. Destroyed bell-bottoms. A loose peasant blouse. Sandals. And some retro sunglasses. Mai had a hippie vibe going on.

"Hello, Janis Joplin," Carson said, looking at the performer emerging. Janis Joplin was a legend in their area. She grew up only a city over, in Port Arthur.

"I know, right? This look is perfect for me, Emma. Great eye," Mai said, looking at her reflection.

"You look great," Emma said, complimenting her friend. "And, you're going to do great. Look, I can't be here. I'm really sorry but—"

"What?!"

Emma turned. She faced Mai.

"You can't? Why not?"

"I'm so sorry. But I have to go. My family needs me today, Mai. You know I wouldn't miss your show for the world, but it's my family."

"She'll be fine. I'll take care of her, Emma. Now go get on that float. We'll see you when the parade's over," Carson said.

The parade floats and marching bands passed through the Texsun City streets. Emma tossed candy to the crowds. From the top of that float, life was great. She snapped a selfie. Not only did the photo capture Emma's joy, it captured many faces in the throngs of people lining the parade route. As she posted it, she knew she had recorded an awesome moment.

Chapter 4

#EmmageMatters

The next morning, Emma couldn't help but go back to her Friender page. She marveled at the amount of attention her Rice Festival pictures were getting. It was as if she were some sort of celebrity. The picture she took from the top of the float was a huge success. *I'm going viral in a minute*, she thought, laughing at herself.

Emma knew Mai's posts would get the

most likes. But her own pictures had actually received the most attention.

She showed her parents. However, they weren't interested in anything that had to do with social media. Especially if it didn't involve the family business. Some of their colleagues were on Friender, but they were not. It wasn't their thing.

"I'm far too busy to keep up with posting consistently," her mother told her.

"My assistant runs my account. I don't even know the password," her father added.

Emma sat down to reply to the comments on her float selfie. She decided on something simple: "It was a beautiful day filled with friends and family." That was just right. The excitement of getting so many likes intrigued her. Even high schoolers were into the photo. Some people even tagged themselves in the crowd behind Emma's image. It seemed like everyone in Texsun City had seen it.

Her phone rang. It was Carson. "You have over five hundred likes on your photo! Are you on Friender right now?"

"Yeah, I'm on," she said, laughing. "Isn't it crazy? It's just a regular old selfie."

"There's nothing regular about it. You nailed that moment. Have you talked to Mai?"

"No, I never know what Elise is filling her head with these days. Let her tell it. I'd be trying to take her shine," Emma said.

"Nah, some things just happen. That post is epic," Carson gushed. "Your stock just hit the roof at SMS. I'll tell you that. Even the quarterback at the high school commented. He said, 'Great pic!' "

"I know! Cray-cray. Well, I have to go. I think I'm on to something over here. I don't want to lose it."

"Huh? What do you have cooking over there, Emma Swanson?"

"You'll find out soon enough, Carson

Roberts. Just stay tuned," Emma said knowingly.

"Hey, wait! Can you pick me up for the meeting today?" Carson asked. "My mom is too busy to drive me."

"I'll ask Mister Victor to pick you up on the way to Elise's. I'll see you soon."

Her parents' business talks echoed in Emma's head. That kicked her brain into overdrive. She knew she couldn't let this moment of popularity pass and not capitalize on it. She had the ears and eyes of her peers. And she planned on turning it into something.

Watching the number of likes grow had been eye-opening. She made notes. She toyed with hashtags. Then it hit her like a runaway train. When she wrote it down, she knew it was right. Staring back at her was the hashtag EmmageMatters. It was everything. It encompassed who she was. She had been ignored by this city for far too long. Finally, people would begin to see her as more than just a Swanson.

Under her iconic picture, she wrote "#EmmageMatters." Then kids started to comment on the hashtag itself.

"Cute!"

"Luv the hashtag!"

Shoot! I'm late, she thought, turning off her iPad. She had been consumed by her new project. Poor Carson! She'd forgotten all about her. They'd be late for sure.

The meeting at Elise's house was to prepare for Mai's next performance. Mai also needed feedback on her Rice Festival show. Miss Arina called their driver, Mr. Victor, to let him know Emma was ready.

Mr. Victor drove to Carson's house, which was more than a little out of the way. They crossed town, then backtracked to Elise's house.

Elise's parents were not considered super wealthy. Though she definitely didn't want for anything. She had just enough to leave her hungry for more.

When they pulled into Elise's gated community, they were given clearance by the security guard. The girls had come here only once before. Elise had given them strict instructions not to ring the doorbell. She had a new baby brother. The nanny would kill her if they woke him up from his nap.

"Y'all have it made," Carson said, looking out the window at Elise's neighborhood. "My mom and I would be in heaven if we had just a small piece of what you have."

Emma thought about it. She had never really looked at her upbringing from Carson's point of view. To her, being a Swanson came with its own baggage. She tried to look at it through Carson's eyes.

"I guess," she mumbled, lost in her own embarrassment.

"You guess? You have a driver. At one point, we didn't even have a car," Carson said.

In Emma's mind, Carson was no different from Elise or Mai. She was smart and beautiful. She dated Holden, the most desired boy in seventh grade. If you asked Emma, Carson was the girl who had it all.

They pulled into a circular driveway. Elise and Mai were waiting on the front porch. Elise hurried them inside. Apparently, the two had already begun to talk about their next move. Elise had edited the video from the Rice Festival. They were in the middle of watching what she had done.

"That's amazing, Elise! You have such a great eye for this," Mai said.

"It's okay. I still have a ways to go. I want perfection. Plus, I want to do a big Internet push," she told them. "Maybe you could give us some tips. You seem to be getting so much attention these days," she said, looking at Emma sternly.

"Who, me?" Emma asked. She looked up from her iPad, flustered to be caught not paying attention.

"Yeah, I mean ... what a clever hashtag. EmmageMatters. Maybe you could think of something like that for Mai. Since you are *so* ... creative."

Emma could tell Elise's comments weren't truly compliments. She was throwing jabs. The whole room became tense, waiting for a reaction. Emma wasn't about to let Elise steal her moment. She was just jealous, and Emma knew it.

It wasn't all about Mai. After all, Elise was an eighth grader. It was her year to be at the top of the food chain. For a brief moment,

Emma Swanson was getting more attention than the student body president. Emma wasn't about to be bothered by her.

"Thanks, Elise. You're a real class act."

Mai jumped in before their thinly veiled insults turned into something major. "Well, I loved the picture. I think it was so cool. You looked beautiful, Emma. The picture spoke for itself."

"Thanks, Mai. Um, there's no time like the present to let y'all know. I do have a little something brewing since that selfie went viral." She hated sharing something so intimate in front of Elise. It would just give her one more thing to be jealous about. "EmmageMatters is here to stay. I'm going to start a thirty-day campaign. See where it takes me. Every day, I'm going to do one post on fashion, food, teen issues. You get the picture, so to speak."

"What do *you* know about fashion, food, or teen issues?" Elise asked her. "You just came out of that little shell you've been in. And now you're an expert? Stay in your lane," Elise warned.

"Elise!" Mai said, shocked. "It's a great idea, Emma. Don't listen to her."

"We'll see about that. You know she hasn't been relevant till now," Elise said. "You took the little shine you got from Mai. Then you turned it into something for yourself. If it wasn't for Mai, people wouldn't even know your name. It's selfish. That's all I'm saying."

"Well, maybe it's time for me to think about myself a little bit. There are girls out there just like me who are going unnoticed," Emma snapped. "Not everyone can be as popular and perfect as you, Elise Mitchell."

Carson finally spoke up. "Look, we all helped each other out during a time when we needed somebody. I was just accepted to Summit. Mai was hiding her talent. Emma was trying to disappear. I support you, Em."

"Thanks, Carson."

"Well, I know one thing. This Emmage-Matters thing better not interfere with Mai's career. The moment it does, you're out. Now, let's focus on the civic center performance. Put the iPad away, Emma," Elise ordered. "We're going to need all hands on deck for this one."

Elise smiled knowingly. She was sure Mai's next performance would be huge.

Chapter 5

Not Just Any Show

Mai wasn't an opening act. She was *the* act. Ticket buyers wanted to see her. She couldn't let them down. It was spring break. The excitement was contagious. The concert was Friday, just as the break officially began.

Students were pumped. Elise had done a massive PR campaign at Texsun City High on Mai's behalf. It looked like she was successful.

Mai had enlisted her cousins, especially

Cara, who was attending Texas A&M. From the number of tickets sold, word had gotten out.

Mai had the talent and the looks. People wanted to support a winner. And her ability to win was undeniable.

Emma and Elise were at Mai's house after school making final changes. Emma was snapping pictures and taking selfies. More selfies than anyone would think humanly possible.

"Come on, Emma," Mai pleaded. "Put the camera away. I need to think. I'm nervous."

"I'm not even taking pictures of you. These are of me."

"Exactly. I need you to focus."

"I told you this would happen," Elise whispered.

"Look, I have everything ready. I'm waiting on y'all. Plus, I know how to multi-task," Emma said.

Mai's mother moved around the house,

getting everything ready. "Let's go, girls!" she yelled. "The hairstylist and makeup artist are already en route to the civic center."

"Yes, ma'am," Elise called. "Let's load 'em up."

Carson met them at the door of the performance hall. She had arrived at the civic center an hour before, waiting on the last props to arrive. "What do you need me to get?" she asked, jumping in to help. "I already set up the opening acts in their dressing areas. They are all here and accounted for. Elise, we need to talk," she said, pulling her to the side.

"What, Carson? Spit it out. You're making me nervous," Elise said.

"It's no big deal, but that girl group? The rappers. They need some help on wardrobe, makeup, and hair. Go and check it out for yourself. They are struggling."

"Look, they sold a lot of tickets. Their

people know what to expect. My only concern is Mai. I can't be bothered with it. Take care of it, Carson. When our stylist gets here, I'll send her over to you."

"Perfect!" Carson said, turning to go to the girl-group's dressing room.

"Hey, Carson!" Elise yelled back at her. "You're doing a great job."

"Thanks, Elise."

Once the concert started, everything went into overdrive. It was unbelievable that middle school students had pulled off this epic event. When it was Mai's turn to perform, everyone was in position.

Before anyone knew it, it was time for the grand finale. Carson was ready. "Drop the ice!" she yelled to Mai's cousins, who were working as stagehands. They did just that.

They waited for Mai's big entrance. But

she did not appear on the stage. They continued to drop more ice as the music played on. Carson cued the lights to dance. The crowd was screaming with anticipation. Carson and Elise were both freaking out. This was not how it was supposed to go. Where was Mai? What was happening?

"What do you mean you don't have the costume? Where is it?!" Mai asked furiously. There was no time for errors.

"I don't know. I thought your mom put it in the truck," Emma said, talking fast.

"I told you to focus. If you had, then I wouldn't be standing here like a fool. There are hundreds of people!"

Elise was by her side. "What is going on?"

"She forgot the costume for the grand finale! That's what!" Mai hissed.

It was Elise's turn to calm Mai down.

"Mai, get over here!" Elise ordered. She

took the sequined top from one outfit and paired it with the pants from another.

Mai was dressed in black. She looked like a chic goth when Elise was done. Elise added black eyeliner and black lipstick to give it the final touch.

"Genius," Mai told her as she ran to the stage. The look made her change the mood of the song. She sang from her soul.

"I have chills," Carson whispered.

"Me too," Elise said, smiling.

Emma felt bad. She could barely watch the performance. It was great, but no thanks to her. She had really messed up. She didn't even feel like listening. She sent Mr. Victor a text, letting him know that she was ready to leave.

Before Mai left the stage, Emma had already slipped out the back door. Good thing it was spring break. She had a little time to get herself together before facing her friends.

The last thing she had wanted was to prove Elise Mitchell right.

Unfortunately, she had done just that. She had embarrassed herself. And she had messed up big-time. She didn't know how she was going to make it up to her best friends.

Chapter 6

Caught in the Middle

After Mai's performance, she wasn't in the mood to discuss Emma's epic fail. Mai knew it could have been a disaster. But the energy from the crowd had been like a healing serum. She wasn't happy with Emma. She wasn't about to go off on her either.

Carson greeted her as soon as she came off the stage. "Another amazing show!"

Elise was emailing videos and snapshots. She never looked up from her iPad.

"Good job, honey! We are on to the next one," Elise said as her fingers flew.

Mai was beaming. She could feel a good performance. This had been just that. "Where's Emma?"

"I don't know," Carson said, puzzled. "I haven't seen her since you went on …" her voice trailed off, realizing what had happened.

"She left? *Humph*." That was all Mai could say. She wasn't about to let Emma ruin her evening.

"Your mom and sister want to get a bite to eat. They're in the audience. I told them we would meet them outside once you were done changing."

"Yes! I'm famished."

In the days that followed, Emma could feel the tension in her group growing. They never talked about the fact that Emma had disappeared during Mai's final act. If they weren't bringing it up, then she definitely wasn't going to.

But there was a huge elephant in the room. Nobody wanted to talk about it. It was the middle of spring break. They didn't have to be around each other. They were trying. Their relationship, however, wasn't flowing.

The girls decided to see a movie. They met in the mall's food court. Emma was the last to show up.

"Hey, my BFF's," she said, moving in to greet her friends. Carson responded warmly. Mai seemed to tense up the closer Emma came to her.

"What's wrong?" Emma asked Mai, who did not respond. "Come on, Mai. Are you still angry about the wardrobe malfunction?"

Mai's eyes were icy cold. She looked up from her corndog. "Really, Emma? Really? First you almost ruin my show. Now you act like it's no big deal."

"Was the show ruined?" Emma asked.

"That's not the point, Em. You and your little hashtag are all that you think about. EmmageMatters, EmmageMatters. We get it! We never thought you didn't matter. *You* thought you didn't matter. Now you're just being obsessive. This time I was caught off guard. I won't let it happen again, though."

"You're just mad because I'm getting more followers. More likes. And more friends than you are."

"Are you serious?" Mai looked to Carson for help.

Carson tried to be helpful. "It's not a competition, Emma. Come on. You know Mai is not like that. The real issue was the fact that you dropped the ball. You really haven't taken ownership of that yet."

"Yes I did. What do the two of you want me to do? How many times do I need to apologize?" Emma asked.

"Once would be nice," Mai said, looking her friend squarely in the eyes.

"Well, I'm sorry. There. Is that good enough? Are you happy, Carson?"

"Huh? I was just saying—"

"Yes, I know. Frankly, I'm done with this whole conversation," Emma said.

Emma decided to do a little retail therapy instead of going to the movies with her friends. She snapped selfies in the dressing room, asking for help from her followers on which sundress she should buy. She had overwhelming support for the black off-the-shoulder dress with colorful flowers.

She went to the shoe department and picked up a pair of black sandals. Perfect. Once she was done shopping, she called Mr. Victor. She was ready to leave. Waiting outside and loaded with shopping bags, she took another selfie. "Bought 2 much. Lawd.

But hey, #EmmageMatters," she posted to her page.

She couldn't stop looking at her Friender. Her number of likes was growing by the second. She loved the attention she was getting. She never thought she was interesting enough for people to tune in to what she was doing. A year ago, this was not possible.

Carson and Mai sat pouting in the mall. They were recovering. It felt like they had been caught up in Hurricane Emma, as they liked to call her. They didn't feel like going to the movie anymore. They picked at their food. And complained.

"She just doesn't get it. Just as important as her hashtag is to her, my singing is to me."

"You cannot compare the two. I'm sorry. That's like comparing apples to oranges. She created a hashtag, for God's sake," Carson muttered. "She takes pictures of herself. Did you see the posts since she bailed? People are voting on dresses for her. What you are doing takes talent, dedication, and hard work."

"Well, it's important to her. She sees it as a stepping-stone to somewhere else."

"You know I know that. I'm just saying … apples to oranges. It's just different."

"Well, they *are* both fruit," Mai said, nudging Carson as they threw their food into the large trash cans.

"Look, I'm going to talk to her. This whole thing has been blown out of proportion. Now that she's finally apologized," Carson said, rolling her eyes. "You two can move forward."

"That was *not* an apology," Mai said.

"I know that and you know that. She doesn't know that. You are just going to have to forgive her. We can't go on like this."

"Okay, but she can't go on acting like a spoiled little attention-craving brat either."

"Well said. I like the way you link your adjectives, but be nice," Carson said.

"You know Father still puts me through drama to even come to the mall. She ruined my outing, and I don't know when I can go out again," Mai said.

"I know. Let's go shopping for a little bit. That'll make you feel better."

Carson tried to call Emma when she got home. But she got her voice mail. She knew Emma did it on purpose. When she opened her Friender page, Emma's latest post was there. Emma was sitting in her room, surrounded by her new swag. The caption read "You mad or nah? #EmmageMatters."

"Ridiculous," Carson said, throwing her phone on the bed. "Just ridiculous."

Chapter 7

Not You Too?

The last thing Emma wanted to do was go back to being on a middle school campus without any friends. If you let Friender tell it, she was the most popular girl at SMS. How could she have so many friends but feel so alone at the same time?

There was one person who she could always count on for the truth. There was one person who never cut her any slack. He always made her laugh. And he was just one text away: Finn Franklin.

To everyone else, he was the class clown. Somewhere along their path, they had formed an actual friendship. It reached beyond the surface of who Finn was and into the heart of the young man she had grown to adore. She sent him a text to see if they could meet up during lunch.

She wanted to meet under the old oak tree in front of the school. In return, he sent her a big thumbs up emoji on FlashChat. Then he sent a selfie. She could feel her insides smile as she saw his big goofy grin.

"Whaddup?" Finn said, joining her at the tree.

It was a perfect day for a little afternoon outdoor lunch. Birds were singing. Winter's chill had been burned away by spring's warmth. There was just enough breeze. And the oak tree's shade took away the sun's glare.

The bench under the tree was a popular spot. She was happy to get first dibs.

"Finn Franklin, it's been too long."

"Well, you know I'm always available for you. You're just so popular these days. I don't know where I fit into your schedule. Thank *you* for making time for the little people."

"You're silly, Finn."

He removed his lunch from a brown paper bag. He had a gigantic submarine sandwich. It made Emma's mouth water. It was already cut in half, so Finn politely put one half on a napkin and gave it to Emma. He took the other half for himself.

"You know, Holden is going to kill me if he finds out I gave you his half of my mom's Italian cold cut."

"Holden will be okay. I'm sure Carson is taking good care of him," she said.

He could see that she had gone to a far-off place just by saying Carson's name.

"*Sooo* …" he asked, trying to jolt her out of her trance.

"So, what?"

"So, why, would be more like it. So, why aren't you eating with Carson and Mai?"

"Can't I just want to have lunch with you, Finn?" He gave her a knowing look. "Okay, okay. We aren't talking right now."

"So the 'You mad or nah?' was for them? I was wondering," Finn said.

"That was bad, huh?" Emma asked.

"Yeah, that's not really something I'd expect from the three of you. What's up with the EmmageMatters hashtag thing you're doing? I mean … I'm not one to pry, but you did invite me to lunch. Your pictures are cute. Don't get me wrong. I just liked them better on FlashChat, when it was for my eyes only. Not just to show how many likes you can get."

"I'm not doing it for likes, Finn."

"Really? Then why?"

"What? I don't know. I mean … everyone else has pictures posted to Friender. My target was for girls like me. The girls who don't get noticed. So they have somebody who they can relate to." She started to feel defensive. She couldn't understand why he was making a big deal out of her pictures when other girls had been posting forever.

"I think it's a good idea, Emma. Just make sure that's what it's for. Not to boost your own self-esteem. You are great just like you are. You don't need all of Summit to tell you that."

"You don't sound like you think it's a good idea," Emma said.

"You are on my newsfeed every time I pick up my phone. Trust me again when I say I don't mind. You are as cute as ever." He reached across the table and tapped her nose, making the blood rush to her cheeks and taking away her anger. "I'm just saying it's a lot. You don't have to try so hard. You don't have to be so *needy*."

The conversation was a roller-coaster ride of emotions. *Needy?* She was angry all over again. "Needy? Are you serious, Finn?" Her eyes landed on the clouds above her. She wished she was up there, jumping from one white pillow to the other. She wished she could escape middle school. It sucked.

She felt tears stinging her eyes.

Finn looked at her coolly.

"I am *not* needy. I have never been. I've always taken the backseat to everyone. I've been the one nobody saw," she cried. "Finally people are starting to notice *me*. I can't believe my friends don't support that."

She got up and left, leaving the sandwich uneaten. Finn had a decision to make: chase after Emma, or eat the rest of that sandwich. He chose the sandwich. At some point, she would see that he was being her friend. If he didn't tell her the truth, then who would? Definitely not the people pretending to like everything she wore, ate, and did.

Sometimes the truth hurts. She'll be back, he said to himself, enjoying the rest of his lunch.

Emma went to the restroom. She ran into a stall. She wanted to be alone. She could let the tears fall.

Not even Finn can make this better, she thought. *Why is everyone against me?*

She had remained a solo entity for a long time. Now she knew what it was like to have friends and be part of something. Being alone now felt different than before. It left an empty place in her heart. She wanted to go back to the old times. Back to Carson and Mai. She just didn't know how to get there.

Chapter 8

Getting In

*E*mma still wasn't talking to her friends. She found any reason to avoid the cafeteria so that she wouldn't have to face them. It was an uncomfortable situation.

Today was different. She went to the library, where she planned to indulge in her favorite book and eat her lunch. She gave the library door a tug, but it was locked. As she read the note on the door, she realized the library was closed for the day. What was she going to do now?

The last thing she wanted to do was get in trouble for roaming the halls. The second to last thing she wanted was to go into the cafeteria. It was the better of two evils, though.

She crept into the cafeteria, trying to go unnoticed. She could see Carson and Mai eating lunch together. Holden and Finn were walking over to their table. She decided to grab the corner table closest to the door. Nobody ever sat there. They wouldn't notice her. Nobody would.

Just as she took out her sandwich, Monroe Harris came strolling through the door. She was co-captain of the cheerleaders. She had taken her place at the top of the totem pole with Jessa McCain still away at TAC, the Texsun City Alternative Center.

Emma's goal was to avoid eye contact.

She didn't want to bring any attention to herself. In true Monroe fashion, she noticed Emma immediately.

"Emma Swanson, what are you doing eating alone?" Her eyes fell on the table where Carson, Mai, Holden, and Finn sat. "Trouble in paradise?" she asked coyly.

Emma could see that Monroe was enjoying the rift. She was going to rub it in her face. After all, it was Emma, Carson, and Mai who had exposed the bullying Jessa, Monroe's best friend.

"You don't have to answer that. I can see for myself. One thing I know is that Emma Swanson cannot eat at a table alone in the cafeteria. That's not kosher."

"You've never cared before, Monroe."

"You're like a star now, Emma. People are starting to use your hashtag under their pictures. It's the latest trend." She took out her phone to show Emma a post from some of the sixth graders who started using her hashtag. One read "#EmmageMatters n so do I."

It was exactly what Emma had wanted. The other girls who had gone unnoticed on campus were stepping out from the shadows. Her friends could say what they wanted. She was making a difference.

"The girl who started this hashtag needs to come and have lunch at our table."

"At the cheerleaders' table? Are you serious?" Emma wasn't buying it. She had tried to be a part of that group twice, but they had shunned her every attempt. Now after all this time, Monroe Harris was inviting her. "What would Jessa say about that?" Emma asked skeptically.

"Jessa has *totally* changed since being at TAC. I'm telling you. It's cool," Monroe said.

Emma was convinced. She gathered her

things and walked over to join Monroe and the others. It felt as though she was walking in slow motion. Carson and Mai appeared to stop talking in midsentence. They looked mesmerized by the scene. Emma held her head just a little bit higher as she took a seat next to Monroe.

Harper could not hold her tongue. "Company?" she asked Monroe.

"Yes," Monroe responded firmly, easing the tension.

"EmmageMatters, huh?" Harper said, looking directly at Emma.

Emma shrugged her shoulders in response. She didn't know what Harper wanted from her. There was no reason to get into a battle of words. Then something happened that Emma didn't expect.

"I've been meaning to tell you that I really like what you're doing. It's cool. I almost created HarperMatters. But it didn't have the same ring to it," she said, half-joking and half-serious.

"Thanks, Harper," Emma said, genuinely surprised that she even knew about her hashtag. The more people started following her posts, the more she knew she was doing the right thing. She was a content creator. If her own friends couldn't see that, then she would have to find friends who could.

"She looks rather cozy over there with them," Mai said, trying not to stare at Emma.

"I can't believe she would stoop so low," Carson added. "Eating with the enemy."

"Well, you didn't leave her many options, did you?" Finn asked them, turning more serious than they had ever seen him.

"What do you mean?" Carson asked him defensively.

"I mean, she talked to me about what

was going on between the three of you. She doesn't feel supported. I don't think I gave her much support either. I'm just as much to blame."

They let his words sink in. Each of them was trying to avoid staring at the cheerleaders' table. The basketball team had joined them. Mai and Carson felt a twinge of envy as they watched Emma interact with her new crowd. They missed their friend.

None of this was lost on Finn. Watching the guys from the basketball team flirt with Emma made him a little hot under the collar. They weren't boyfriend and girlfriend or anything, but there *was* a connection. He couldn't imagine her giving that attention away to someone else.

"Holden, let's see what the guys are doing outside," he said, wanting to separate himself from the scene.

"Cool. It's getting heavy in here anyway."

"Wait, you're not leaving us," Carson said.

"Yeah, it's a beautiful day. I want out of these four walls," Mai added.

Carson and Mai couldn't resist looking back one last time at Emma. She had been looking at them too. Each of them turned their heads away as they put more distance between the drama.

Chapter 9

Just My Emma-gination

It had been two weeks since Emma started hanging out with Monroe, Harper, and the other cheerleaders. The uneasiness she once felt being around them was slowly starting to leave.

"You know cheerleading tryouts are coming up again," Monroe told her on the way to the cafeteria.

"Yeah, I saw the flyers in the hallway."

"Are you going to try out?" Monroe asked.

"I hadn't thought about it." Emma immediately became uneasy. She had tried out two years in a row and had not made it. Monroe had been there at each tryout. She had watched as Emma bombed repeatedly.

"Well, I think you should. If you need help, I'll work with you."

"Thanks, Monroe. I'll think about it."

They had really become close in the past two weeks. Emma enjoyed hanging out with her. She reminded her of Carson. They had the same chestnut skin color and brown eyes. Monroe straightened her hair. She was not the kind of girl to go natural like Carson.

Monroe looked like she enjoyed whipping her ponytail while she was cheering. She had the most spirit of all the girls. If it wasn't for Jessa McCain, she would definitely be captain. Jessa had a way of forcing herself to the top of the pecking order. It was not in her nature to follow. Monroe was too mellow to go against her best friend. Emma really liked Monroe. She just wondered what would happen when Jessa returned from TAC.

They walked into the cafeteria and ran smack-dab into Carson and Mai. Emma stood frozen in her tracks. Automatically, her mouth opened to say hello. But she closed it, remembering that they were still angry. None of this was lost on Monroe. She slipped her arm through Emma's. They moved past the girls without saying a word.

"Awkward," she whispered to Emma as they joined the cheerleaders at their table.

"Yeah, thanks," Emma said, looking back over her shoulder to sneak a peek at her friends.

"What kind of purse was Emma carrying?" Mai asked Carson.

"Tell me you didn't miss her good-morning selfie. It's Chanel, darling."

"She's dripping in labels now. Ugh. Just like them," Carson said. "She swore this hashtag thing was supposed to be empowering. But I think she's stroking her own ego."

"Or lack thereof. Come on, this is crazy. That's not our Emma. If she was uplifting other girls, then it wouldn't be all about labels. This is like a 'have or have not' campaign."

"At least you're part of Team Have. I don't know, Mai. She's changed. With everything that has gone your way, you are still the same Mai."

"I don't know how to change, Carson. I've never wanted to be part of their little clique. Emma's always wanted that. I wouldn't put it past her if she tried out for cheerleading again this year."

"I never thought about that. But you are *so* right. Well, I wish her luck. If she's happy, then so be it."

Carson checked her phone. She forgot that she had received a text last period. She was slow to take it out in class. Some of the teachers would take phones on sight.

"Omigod! Omigod!"

"What?" Mai asked her worriedly.

She shoved her phone in Mai's hand and watched her reaction. Mai's mouth flew open. Her eyes looked as though they would pop out of her head.

"Do you think that's really Emma?" Carson asked as she studied the picture.

"Nah. It can't be. Emma would never."

"Don't finish that sentence, because you don't know."

The realization that their friendship with Emma would never be the same was slowly starting to sink it. The fact that she had changed and there was no going back was becoming obvious.

Emma thought people were staring at her. Or maybe it was her imagination. It was as though the whole cafeteria was in on the same joke.

When the basketball team came over to the cheerleaders' table after finishing their food, she was getting *way* more attention than usual. They were fussing over who would sit next to her. It was weird. Only the day before, she was just a regular girl. Now they were acting like she was a supermodel.

She leaned over toward Monroe. "What is really going on today?"

"Girl, you're complaining. You must be the flavor of the month. There's always a new one," she said, laughing.

"I guess, but something feels off."

She looked up to see Finn staring at her. When their eyes met, he walked out of the cafeteria. *What was that about?*

For a second, she wanted to go after him. She wanted to understand what was happening.

"Hey, what are you doing this week-end?" the captain of the basketball team was asking her.

"I don't know," she said, shrugging her shoulders.

"We should hang out," he told her.

Just then the bell rang, ending lunch. Saved by the bell was an understatement. Emma distanced herself as quickly as possible from the knowing looks and winks, from the giggles, the kids pointing in her direction. The normal gossip of middle school had gone wild. And Emma was in the epicenter of it all.

Chapter 10

In Hot Water

Emma loved her ceramics class. With a crazy day like the one she was having, she needed some peace. She asked Mr. Blanton if she could work on the pottery wheel in the back of the classroom. It was tucked away to give students creative space. Nobody bothered you there. There was a no-talking rule that was understood.

She put her apron on and weighed her clay. When she had just the right amount, she began to knead and prepare it, making sure there were no air bubbles that could mess up her masterpiece. She placed her prepared clay on the wheel and dipped her hands into the water pot next to her.

Turning the wheel on a slow speed, she molded the clay just right, losing herself in the process. She dipped her hands in the water again and went back to work. As she began to pull at the sides of the clay, she could see the pot forming before her eyes. It was going to be perfect.

Emma stopped the wheel. She took out the string she used to cut the base of the pot off the wheel. But she was startled by another presence that had entered the small space. It was Gemma Spell, the office assistant.

"Hey, Gemma. How are you? What are you doing in here?"

"The principal wants to see you."

"Me? Why?"

She handed a pass to Emma without another word. Emma was being summoned by the principal. That had never happened before. *Am I getting an award? Am I in trouble?*

She finished up and removed her pot from the wheel, took off her apron, and headed toward Mr. Blanton. "They want to see me in the office. I left my vase in the wheel area. It's ready to go into the kiln for the next round."

"I'll give it a look when I go back there. I'm putting pots in the kiln after school. I'll let you know when it's ready for painting."

"Thanks, Mister Blanton."

Her thoughts were scattered as she walked down the hall to the principal's office. She could not guess what this was about. The best she could do was figure it out before she sat down across from Principal Buckley.

As soon as she walked in the door, the

principal's secretary told her she could go in. This had to be one of the oddest days of her life. At least she was smart enough to know this meeting was not going to be good.

"Close my door, Miss Swanson," Principal Buckley said to her.

"Yes, ma'am," Emma said, smiling nervously.

"So how are you doing at Summit this year, Emma?"

"Oh, I'm having a great year."

"You know I've been keeping up with your hashtag, EmmageMatters. That was your idea, right?"

"Oh yes, ma'am. I'm very proud of it. As you know, I've been pretty shy. This is the first year that I've been able to break out of my shell. Hashtag EmmageMatters was a way of letting other girls my age know they can do the same."

Emma was proud of herself. She thought

she was being called into the office for something she'd done wrong. Instead, Mrs. Buckley wanted to let her know she was one of her
followers. This wasn't turning out to be such
a bad day after all.

"Well, for the most part, I like it. There is
just one thing that concerns me."

*Oh no! Is she about to call me self-
absorbed too? When does this end?* Emma
braced herself. She wasn't about to let this
end the way that it had with Finn.

"What concerns you?" Emma asked.

"I don't know how else to put it. We don't
tolerate provocative pictures on this campus.
It's been brought to my attention that one of
your images has been reported as containing
inappropriate content."

"No, that must be a mistake."

Mrs. Buckley turned her computer
screen toward Emma. Emma thought her
eyes would pop out of her head. The image

in front of her was her face. But it definitely was not her body.

"That's not me," Emma said, shaking her head vigorously.

"Emma, that definitely is you."

Emma was shocked. She couldn't believe it. How could Mrs. Buckley believe she was capable of something like that?

"No, ma'am. I would never."

"Well, until I know for a fact that this is not your photo, I'm going to have to suspend you."

"Suspend me?" She couldn't believe her ears. "Surely there's an explanation for this. I need to call my mother."

"Your mother has already been notified. She should be here shortly to take you home pending the investigation. We can't have you on campus right now. You are a distraction to the other students. Also, I need you to take that photograph down immediately if you plan on returning to Summit. Am I clear?"

"Yes, ma'am." Emma hung her head in shame. Someone had done this to her. Targeted her. It was malicious and it hurt. "May I use the restroom?" she asked.

"Of course. Use mine. The students will transition to their next class soon. I don't want you in the hallway."

She was being treated like a leper. She went into the principal's private restroom. All of the emotions she had experienced today overwhelmed her. She felt the tears run down her face. She wished that her mother had already arrived.

Surely Mom won't believe this. Surely she'll be on my side. Emma didn't think she could take any more heartbreak, not right now. She just needed somebody to have her back. To be on her side.

Chapter 11

No Laughing Matter

Her mother was dressed like she had just walked away from a *Vogue* photo shoot. She looked out of place in the school with her white Dior pantsuit and expensive high heels. Her red hair fell in loose waves. Her makeup was flawless.

Emma was happy to see her until their eyes met. Her mother looked at her like she didn't know who she was. Emma could only assume that Principal Buckley had filled her in over the phone. She just hoped that her mother hadn't bought into the lies.

"I'm sorry I'm late. I was caught in a meeting."

"That's fine, Mrs. Swanson. We talked about some of the details over the phone."

"Yes, ma'am. But it's still hard for me to believe that there were provocative pictures of *my* daughter on the Internet. Emma is just starting to warm up to the camera. Just last Christmas we were begging her to get in the family photos."

"Things do change a lot at this age, Mrs. Swanson. Has Emma shared her Internet campaign? It's called EmmageMatters."

"No, I am not aware of it. Emma, what is Mrs. Buckley talking about?"

"Mom, you know I have been taking more pictures."

"I'm confused, Emma. So, what she's telling me is true about you and the photos?"

"Yes … I mean no. Mom, come on. You *know* me. I would never do anything to embarrass our family. The pictures I took were of food, clothes, makeup. Stuff like that. Not lingerie." She lowered her voice to a whisper, as if she had said a dirty word. "I don't even own lingerie."

Her mother examined her daughter's face. Emma had never been good at lying. She always gave herself away. When she was five, her mother found her favorite makeup empty. Emma was called to her room. She denied ever touching it. But her guilty look gave her away. Plus, she had forgotten to clean up the evidence. Makeup-filled towels were everywhere in her bathroom.

Then there was the broken high-heel shoe. And the snack that disappeared. Each time, she had been caught in a lie. In those moments, Emma had learned that lying wasn't for her. She couldn't cover her tracks.

Needless to say, Mrs. Swanson knew when her daughter was being less than honest. At this moment, she was not.

"Emma, you really need to tell your mother the truth at some point. Mrs. Swanson, an infraction like this carries a heavy consequence. Your daughter could be suspended for three days and put on probation. I've already given her strict instructions to remove the picture."

"A three-day suspension? Emma has never been in trouble before in her life. I need to see this photograph."

Mrs. Buckley began working to load the photo. "This is middle school, Mrs. Swanson. Emma is in the seventh grade. You have to keep a close watch on her. She is changing every day."

Mrs. Buckley turned her computer screen so that Mrs. Swanson could see the photo for herself. It was definitely Emma's face. Her mother knew at first glance that it was not her daughter's body. She took a deep breath before she began speaking. Emma could tell her mom was angry.

"You call me in here for this? That is not my daughter," she said, trying to control her anger. She glared at the principal.

"How do you know that?"

"Why would you even ask?" Mrs. Swanson snapped. "A mother knows. I guarantee you, with a little more research, you could have found the original picture on the Internet somewhere. That's probably one of those reality TV girls. Look at Emma, and then look at that body again." Her mother laughed. "This is ridiculous, Mrs. Buckley."

"Well, maybe Emma is the one who created the image. Did you think of that?"

"With all due respect, Mrs. Buckley, I would never do that. I don't need that much attention. That's just embarrassing," Emma said with passion.

"The whole hashtag thing, Emma, is a bit on the needy side. I've seen it more times than I'd like to admit. Girls who do what you are doing tend to do anything to get the attention they crave."

"Well, that's not me," Emma said defensively.

"Hm, it looks like the image has already been blocked. But you know this, and so do I. Once it's out there, it's hard to stop it from spreading. Be mindful of what you are doing, Emma." She turned her attention to Mrs. Swanson. "I'm still going to send her home with you today. Her presence has been such a distraction in the classroom, hallways, and cafeteria. I've been monitoring on the cameras, and I think it's for the best."

"I understand, Mrs. Buckley. I'll definitely look into this hashtag a little deeper. I'll have a talk with Emma this evening. Thanks for everything."

"No problem. Are you okay, Emma?"

"I'll be fine, Mrs. Buckley. I guess I have some thinking to do."

"That sounds like a great idea," the principal said.

Chapter 12

Look Who's Back

The next day, Emma wanted to put the whole mess behind her. It felt like she had lived a nightmare. Now she was ready to wake up. When she got to first period, she was tempted to sit by Carson and Mai. She needed them like she needed air to breathe. She missed her friends, but she wasn't in the mood to be shunned. She couldn't handle it today. So instead, she grabbed her normal seat close to the board and took out her homework.

Her mind raced. Even though the picture on the Internet wasn't actually her, she was still embarrassed. She wanted to skip school today. But what good would it have done? She would still have to return. She almost wished she were suspended. Then she would have a valid reason to stay home.

The English teacher was discussing *The Strange Case of Dr. Jekyll and Mr. Hyde*. She could hear the conversation going on around her, but she wasn't interested. She had loved the beginning of the story. Now, nothing seemed important except the fact that she had become the butt of someone's cruel joke.

She walked around in a daze until lunchtime. When she arrived at the table with Monroe and the other girls, there was a new vibe. She could feel it.

"Hey, Monroe," she said solemnly,

sitting down. She looked at the faces around her. Something was up.

The lunchroom fell silent. Emma heard an all-too-familiar voice say, "What the heck?" When she looked up, there was Jessa McCain staring back at her. "Why is she at *my* table? I'm totally confused."

"Jessa, I told you a lot has changed since you've been gone," Monroe said.

"Right, but you didn't say you got all buddy-buddy with the very girl who sent me to TAC in the first place."

"You sent yourself to TAC." The words fell from Emma's lips before she could stop herself. Oh, Lord! What have I done? The last thing she was up for was a run-in with Jessa McCain.

Jessa's eyes narrowed as she zeroed in on Emma. "Monroe, a word," she said.

When the two walked away from the

table, Emma stood up to leave. There was no way she was sticking around to go another round with Jessa.

Harper was quick to stop her. "You don't have to go."

"Look, I'm not trying to cause any drama. I'm not in a good place right now. I can't be around Jessa. She's too much."

"I'm too what?" Jessa asked, coming around the corner. "I'm trying to be calm here. But you are making this rather difficult."

"I'm not trying to. Like you said, this is your table. Have at it," Emma said.

Jessa turned to her friends. "I've been gone for one month. You had to stoop this low. We have not lowered our standards so much as to have Emma Swanson hang out with us. Oh no!"

Monroe tried to step in. "Jessa, please. That's enough."

"You were supposed to keep our group

together, Monroe. I am truly disappointed," Jessa said matter-of-factly.

Emma walked away. She had to get away from Jessa. Away from Monroe. Away from Harper. Her real friends, Carson and Mai, would never have let her get handled the way she just did. She passed their table on her way out of the cafeteria. She couldn't look at them. She tried to avoid eye contact. But she could feel them looking at her. She felt their pity. They had witnessed every humiliating minute.

She ran into a restroom stall and prepared to stay there for the entire afternoon. Gone was the confident girl from EmmageMatters. The only thing left was a shell of a person. She didn't want to look her friends. She didn't want to look at herself either.

What she wanted was to separate from this place. From who she was. And from everything around her. It was as if the whole school was starting to close in on her. The walls were smothering the life from her body. To breathe, she knew she needed to get away.

After the bell rang and the students were tucked away in their classes, she escaped to the nurse's office. She called Miss Arina, who was there in ten minutes.

When her nanny got there, she told her the whole horrible story. Miss Arina held her in her arms and comforted her like she did when she was five. Finally! Somebody who was truly on her side. There was nothing like the comforting arms of her nanny. It just felt like home.

Chapter 13

The White Flag

It was first period, the only class that Carson, Mai, and Emma had together. Emma sat alone. She had been through so much. It had been days since she posted on Friender. There were no more FlashChat messages.

"I can't keep watching her like this. It's breaking my heart," Carson whispered to Mai.

"What can we do? She made it clear that she doesn't want to be friends with us."

"She never actually said that."

"No, but it was clear."

When the bell rang, they wound up right behind Emma. But she was trying to go unnoticed. Emma could sense their presence. She turned around. For a second, there was a connection. Then she turned back abruptly.

Carson nudged Mai. It would have to be her call. She was the one who had the initial problem with Emma. It was up to her to determine how this was going to play out. Before they reached the classroom door, Mai reached out and grabbed Emma's arm. But Emma never turned around. Her body grew stiff. It was as though she didn't know how to respond.

"Emma, are you okay?" Mai whispered to her friend as gently as she could.

Emma slid her hand down and grabbed Mai's. She held it until they were in the hallway. She ducked around a corner, dragging Mai and Carson with her. Once they were out of the moving stream of students, Emma let out a sigh. A tear rolled down her cheek.

"Don't. It's okay," Carson told her. "Let's go to the restroom."

They crossed the crowded hallway, hoping to get some privacy. Luckily, the restroom was clearing out. The bell would be ringing soon. This conversation wasn't something that could be avoided. They had to get past this. Emma was hurting.

"I'm sorry," Emma said to both of her best friends.

"No, we should have been there for you. Been more supportive," Mai told her.

"I turned into a mini-monster. Everything happened so fast. I don't know."

"Truth moment. You were more like a

big monster," Carson said, nodding her head. Mai nudged Carson in the arm. "Just sayin'," Carson added.

"I know. But I felt like the two of you abandoned me. I felt like I had no support when I tried to step out and do something for myself. Where my girls at?" she asked, taking a line from Beyoncé.

"I get that," Mai told her. "I'll own it. I'm sorry too."

"But, Mai, I owe you the biggest apology. It's one thing to mess up your concert," Emma confessed. "It's a whole other thing to bail like I did."

"Now that … I didn't understand that. I can't lie," Mai said.

"I just couldn't face you after what I'd done. I knew I was wrong. And I would have to hear Elise's lecture. I needed some air. Then, I just called for Mister Victor to come and pick me up," Emma said. "It was like I

couldn't go back in. Then I was so embarrassed when I saw y'all over spring break.
It was like everything had changed. I didn't
know how to fix it."

"You know we can talk about anything.
Bailing is never an option. Okay?" Mai asked.

"It'll never happen again," Emma said,
giving Mai a tight hug. "Now we have to get
a pass before it's way too late. I'm already on
thin ice for that photo."

Carson stopped them from walking
out. "Okay, so that photo wasn't really you,
right?"

"That's the worst question. Ever. No, of
course that wasn't me!"

"Look, I had to ask. You were out there
flossing. You never know," Carson said.

"Okay, last thing," Mai told them. "We
didn't even get to talk about the fact that the
Wicked Witch of Summit has returned."

"Omigod, Jessa hasn't changed at all.

She's still the most awful individual to walk the earth," Emma told them. "I can't stand her. She is horrible."

"You two had it out the other day, huh?" Mai asked her as they walked to the front office.

"Yeah, it wasn't pleasant. She's just—"

"A nightmare," Carson finished for her.

"Exactly!" Mai and Emma said together.

"I've missed you so much," Mai said.

"Me too, Mai. Me too," Emma said.

Chapter 14

The Grand Finn-ale

*E*mma was starting to feel like her old self again. When her friendship with Carson and Mai was jeopardized, she realized they were responsible for her confidence. She couldn't believe she had almost blown it. Her actions almost lost her the two best people in her life.

The only thing that was missing now was Finn. She scoured the whole school looking for him. She couldn't go home before making it right with him too.

It was the last period of the day. There was no telling where Finn was hiding. He had a permanent pass from his teachers. Everyone knew Finn could finish his assignments in minutes. She was lucky when she found him in the gym playing basketball. He was at the far end of the court playing one-on-one with somebody.

The closer Emma came to the court, the more she could make out that the somebody was female. Instantly, she regretted coming here. She took a seat in the stands and waited.

This was a bad idea. Maybe that's his new girlfriend, Emma thought.

About five minutes passed. Finn finished his game and picked up a white towel. He wiped the sweat from his face. Then he walked over to her. He had never looked better than at that moment.

It was as if he were moving in slow

motion. Emma was temporarily at a loss for words.

"Hey, Emma, what brings you to these parts?" Finn asked.

"I just wanted to—I don't know—talk. Are you busy?"

"If you don't mind a little sweat, I'm good." He flashed his award-winning smile.

"I don't mind," she said, smiling uneasily. There was a moment of silence before Emma looked up at him. Her eyes said everything before she could utter a word. "I just want to apologize for … for messing up our friendship."

"Em, we're good. You know me."

"I know, Finn. But I don't want you to think I'm taking you for granted. You're the only person besides Carson and Mai who get me. I never want to mess that up."

"We will always be friends, Emma."

In a flash, Finn was took off his sweaty

shirt. He began to beat his fists on his chest like a gorilla. Emma was mortified. She didn't know what he was doing. "Now come, woman, give me hug!" It was the worst Tarzan impression she had ever seen, but it made her laugh.

"I'm not hugging your sweaty self. You are not—"

He charged after her, sending her running up and down the bleachers. She lost her breath on the last step. He caught her as she gasped between laughs.

She yelled and protested, but he was all over her.

"You are so smelly!" she said giggling. "Stop! Please. Dang, Finn. Go shower!" she said, walking backward out of the gym. She kept her eye on him as she moved.

"I'll be back for more," he said, wiggling his eyebrows.

She giggled all the way to her locker,

rolling her eyes at the thought of what they must have looked like. Finn! He was truly a different being. She was happy because he had forgiven her.

Emma met up with Mai and Carson back at their lockers.

"Why are you cheesing so much?" Carson asked her.

"Uh-huh, she is. Isn't she?" Mai said.

"I am not cheesing," Emma answered, trying to wipe the grin off her face. "Okay, okay, I just finished talking to Finn."

"Finn? That's why you're grinning like that?" Carson asked.

"You said you didn't like him," Mai said.

"I don't like-like him. We are just really good friends," Emma said.

"Girl, I'm your friend. You never look like that after we talk," Mai said.

"For real," Carson added, laughing at

Mai's words. Carson suspected Emma liked Finn more than she was admitting. Even to herself.

"Hey, give me a break. He's a really cute friend," Emma joked. She didn't know if she was ready for anything else. Or if Finn was even interested in her like that. But she warmed up just thinking about it.

"Don't worry," Mai told her. "Something tells me he likes you too. And not just as a really good friend."

Chapter 15

Moving Forward

Mai, Carson, and Emma decided they were due for some much needed girl time. Emma's house was better than Disneyland. So that's where they went on Friday afternoon. Miss Arina had them all set: snacks, movies, and spa-night essentials.

"This is the life. I'm soaking my feet in essential oils. My eyes are relaxing under soothing cucumber slices," sighed Mai.

"I'm glad y'all are both here," Emma admitted.

"I am too," Carson said.

"Truth moment?" Emma asked, removing the cucumbers from her eyes. Carson and Mai removed theirs too. A truth moment had to be done with eye contact or it wasn't real. "I am still really sorry. I know I apologized already. I can't get over how I acted. It was all about me. That's just not right. I almost ruined the two best relationships I've ever had. Nothing is worth that."

"Aw, Em. Truth?" Mai asked her. "I was mad, true. I just knew this wasn't over. I knew we would find our way back to each other. I'm just glad it happened sooner rather than later."

"Me too! I mean, Miss Arina does a first-class sleepover. It makes it so much easier to forgive you," Carson said, laughing.

Emma tossed a small pillow directly at Carson, popping her in the mouth.

"Okay, last question, and then we can go back to our spa. I'm sure enjoying mine. Mai, is your dad actually chilling out on letting you go to sleepovers? What's up with that?" Carson asked.

"You know, he trusts Miss Arina. He knows the Swansons go out of town a lot. Miss Arina is almost as tough as he is. They've had some strange meeting of the minds."

"He talks to Miss Arina?" Carson gasped.

"He talks to everyone who has contact with his children," Mai said. "He's worse with my little sister."

"How can he be worse?" Carson asked. "Hey, can one of you do my eyebrows after this? I need a little changeup."

"Sure," Emma told her. "I'm a beast on the tweezers."

They were enjoying themselves. Listening to music. They video chatted with some of their friends and prank called others. Then they watched a movie. They all agreed it was a dream evening.

Once they got into bed, they talked about everything going on in their lives. Carson couldn't hold it anymore. She had to say something to Emma about her hashtag.

"Look, Emma, you need to start posting again with your hashtag."

"Nah, I'm done with that," Emma said.

"No, Em! You can't be," Mai told her.

"We'll help you with whatever you need."

"As long as the likes don't start going to your head again," Mai added.

Emma thought about it for a minute. She had a lot of followers. There were many kids interested in what she was doing. Even her parents were onboard after going through her posts with a fine-tooth comb. They were mostly pleased.

After the negative feedback and doctored post, she'd become jaded. Now her friends were telling her it was a good idea. What she'd done was worth supporting.

"Wait a minute. So you're telling me that you like EmmageMatters."

"Of course we do," Carson told her. "How could we not? It's all about our girl."

"You are amazing! And you have your mother's sense of fashion. Come on. It's hot!"

"I thought you both hated it."

Emma began to realize how much of a jerk she had been. That wasn't going to happen again. She would never ignore her friends. Slowly she smiled. Her friends were supporting her. "I'm going to take this further than a hashtag. I'm telling you, EmmageMatters is going to be huge one day."

"Yes! That's my girl," Carson told her.

"Just remember the little people when you go national," Mai chimed in.

"Together, we can do anything we put our minds to. Carson, you helped us figure out who we are. I don't know how many times I can say thank you for coming to Summit."

"Trust me. You were my life raft too. What would I do without you?" Carson said.

The three friends were back together again. The problems they faced were speed bumps, not roadblocks. They didn't let it define their friendship. Or their future. Instead, they used it to make their relationship stronger.

There was nobody like a best friend. They were lucky. They each had two.

Want to Keep Reading?

About the Author

Shannon Freeman

Born and raised in Port Arthur, Texas, Shannon Freeman is an English teacher in her hometown. As a full-time teacher, Freeman stays close to topics that are relevant to today's teenagers.

Entertaining others has always been a strong desire for the author. Living in

California for nearly a decade, Freeman enjoyed working in the entertainment industry, appearing on shows like *Worst-Case Scenario*, *The Oprah Winfrey Show*, and numerous others. She also worked in radio and traveled extensively as a product specialist for the Auto Show of North America. These life experiences, plus the friendships she made along the way, have inspired her to create realistic characters that jump off the page.

Today she enjoys a life filled with family. She and her husband, Derrick, have four beautiful children: Kaymon, Kingston, Addyson, and Brance. Their days are full of family-packed events. They also regularly volunteer in their community.

Freeman's debut series, *Port City High*, is geared to high-school readers. When asked to write for middle school students, she knew it would be a challenge, but one that she was up for. *Summit Middle School* is the author's second series. She hopes these stories will reach students from many different backgrounds. "It is definitely a series where middle-grade students can read about realistic life experiences involving characters just like them. Middle school can be a challenge, and if I can help students navigate through that world, then I have met my goal."

Freeman loves writing a series that her children and numerous nephews and nieces can enjoy.